MAX AND RUFUS

Written and Illustrated by Joan Drescher

Houghton Mifflin Company   Boston   1982

To Kim D., who asked, "What if I were a dog?"

To Lyn H., who helped me answer that with
doggedness and caring

Printed in the United States of America

Y 10 9 8 7 6 5 4 3 2 1

Library of Congress Cataloging in Publication Data
Drescher, Joan E.
    Max and Rufus.

    Summary: A dog, Rufus, and his boy, Max, agree to
change places for a while.
    [1. Dogs—Fiction. 2. Humorous stories] I. Title.
PZ7.D78384Max   [E]   82-3061
ISBN 0-395-32435-1   AACR2

MAX AND RUFUS

I have a boy. His name is Max.

He was tired of school buses, washing his ears, and being told to go to bed at eight.

I'm Rufus.

I was sick of being
put out when company came,

flea powder,

and (ugh) dog food.

So one day we made a deal.
He'd be Rufus and I'd be Max.

But being a dog isn't easy. First I
had to teach Max how to act like a dog.
He had to learn how to dig for bones,

fetch the newspaper,   scratch for fleas,

and, of course, bark at the mailman.

Some things Max learned easily.
For one, he never had accidents
on the rug like I do.

Max taught me to blow bubbles,

sit at the table,

take out the trash
(I don't mind the smell the way Max does),

and turn on the TV. I love cartoons!

The first day I took Max
for a walk before breakfast.

He didn't like the leash, but I said,
"Be a good dog," and out we went.

After school Max was waiting for me
at the bus stop.

We'd both had a good day.

I made the baseball team

and Max messed around with my old pals.

The next day I played in the big game.

I caught some great fly balls.

Our team won, and we all went to Sadie's for sodas.

I loved sleeping in Max's bed,
and Max got to stay up as late as he wanted.

Some nights I don't think he
ever went to sleep.

There were days when he did look
awfully tired. Soon, he wouldn't eat

his table scraps, and he stopped coming
to meet me at the bus.

Then he had a hard time keeping up with the other dogs,
and I knew he was in for trouble.

Like the day the gang all ran off with the franks...

Max was the only one who got caught.

They took him off to the pound.

Poor Max, it was a day and a half before he was out!

I liked my new life so much,
but I was worried about Max.

Being a boy wasn't much fun with him
so unhappy. Still, a deal was a deal.

Then one day Max crawled under the sofa and wouldn't come out.

Poor guy, now I really knew how he felt.

"I know a deal is a deal," I said, "and there's never been a better dog than you, but please, Max, come out from under the sofa and be a boy."

Well, what do you bet he did. So now I'm back to scratching fleas and digging for bones, and Max is back to school buses and washing his ears.

But every once in a while
Max will put on my collar
and scare the mailman out of his wits.

And every once in a while I will put on
his hat and sit in the blue velvet
chair in the living room.